GAMERS, HACKERS, AND LIARS

A Novella

Blair Shatzel

CONTENTS

Chapter 1

The day began to grow darker and darker as Burke still sat on the couch, feet propped on the coffee table, a gaming controller in his hands. He reached up and slowly pried his headphones off his head, rubbing his sore ears. He couldn't wait to order the new luxury memory foam padded gaming headphones. At least *those* would still be comfortable even after five hours of playing video games.

Burke set his controller next to him and rubbed his eyes. He looked across the room towards the window, squinting to get a better look at the gloomy street outside. A single street lamp dimly illuminated his front lawn. Burke could hear the distinct sound of his mom's car engine as it rounded the corner.

The glare of headlights momentarily blinded Burke's already dry eyes. He squinted through the window, waiting for his mom to pull up. The garage door slammed and she came into the living room, her high heels tapping on the tiles. Burke's mom looked around the room, eyeing the shoes that had randomly been tossed into opposite corners. With a slight grimace, she strode over to the television and pulled the plug out of the wall.

"C'mon, Mom! Five more minutes, please?" Burke complained, his fingers still positioned on the control buttons. He made his best puppy eyes and stuck out his bottom lip, quivering it just slightly. She shook her head and said with a sigh, "Please go clean your room. You spend way too much time on that thing."

Burke threw his controller onto the couch and started to stomp away.

"Hey!" His mom called after him. "Did you just throw that?" She gave him an accusing glare.

"Sorry, it slipped!" Burke lied. "I accidentally dropped it." He held his hands up in innocence.

"Right," she said with a hint of sarcasm. "Go clean up your room."

"Why do I have to clean my room anyway?" Burke whined. "It's my room and I can do whatever I want with it!"

His mother cleared her throat and shifted from foot to foot. "Well..." She hesitantly started to say, then seemingly changed her mind "Never mind. Just know that anything can happen." She turned on her heels and walked out the door.

What's that supposed to mean? Burke thought as he trudged up the stairs.

Chapter 2

After a whole week of public school torture, Burke finally rounded the corner to his house on a late Friday afternoon. He had his weekend sanctuary in his sights and wasn't about to let the thought of his past-due homework drag him down. He looked around at the neighborhood. Something seemed different. Burke noticed a moving truck in front of the Meyers' yard. They had cardboard moving boxes in their lawn, which flowed over onto Burke's lawn. Burke shrugged. The Meyers were never home anyway, so he didn't really care that they were moving. He took a shortcut through the lawn and dodged the boxes. Burke took the porch steps in one leap and skipped inside. Nothing was going to get in the way of his weekend gaming plans. He tossed his backpack on the couch and plopped next to it. Cracking his knuckles, he stretched his neck and grabbed his controller from beside him. Burke sighed with relief. The week was finally over and he had a full two days to recover.

There was only one small problem, the TV was gone. Burke almost let out a scream. He looked around the room, the TV was definitely missing. That's when he noticed that the dining table was also gone. Along with many other furniture pieces in his house. Burke frantically spun around. Had they been robbed or something? He ran up the stairs to his mom's office and burst through the door, out of breath.

"What happened?" He panted, looking around her office and noticing missing furniture as well. She slowly turned in her chair and looked at Burke with her eyebrows raised.

"What is it, Burke?" She asked with an annoyed look.

"The TV's gone! The furniture's gone! Where is everything?" Burke said, practically shouting.

"Burke, would you please keep your voice down, I'm clearly doing some work here."

Burke clenched his fists and tensed his jaw in exasperation. "You didn't answer the question! Where is the stuff?" Burke tightened his face with anger. "Everyone is ruining my weekend!" He threw his arms up and stormed out of his mom's office, not even waiting for her reply.

Burke decided to go to his room. At least he could still play on his computer. He flung open his door and looked around. Was any of his stuff missing? Burke slumped into his gaming chair, he wasn't even in the mood for virtual combat anymore. He stared blankly at his computer and let his fist fall onto the desk with a loud bang.

"Burke!" He heard from downstairs. He scowled at the door, his mom was always ruining his weekends.

△ △ △

Burke rifled through the cabinets in the kitchen, looking for his secret stash of cheese puffs. "Mom!" He groaned when he found that all the cabinets were empty. He slammed the cupboard door so hard that it almost fell off its hinges.

"Burke! Don't break anything else, or we'll never sell this house!" His mother yelled from the living room. Burke froze.

"What exactly are we selling?" he asked and slowly turned. Burke's mom didn't say anything, but he heard her whisper something to his dad.

"Burke, we realize what you must be thinking. But you have to be open-minded about this."

Burke laughed out loud. He looked at his parents and saw their serious faces, realizing they weren't joking.

"Is this because I didn't clean my room well? Or is this some kind of cruel punishment?"

"No!" Burke's mom, said as she shook with laughter. "We have been building our new house for a while. Your father and I have always wanted to live in the countryside. We want you and Sally to experience nature. It's fifteen miles from the nearest town!"

"What? Is that supposed to be a good thing?"

"Construction on the new house was just completed a few days ago." She explained as if that were a logical answer.

"And why couldn't you tell me this before?" Burke began to raise his voice.

"We wanted it to be a surprise! There is no need to get upset, Burke. This is going to be great." She said cheerfully again.

Burke stared at her, "A surprise?! How is this supposed to be a surprise?"

She smiled again, "It's a nice house! And you'll have a big room!" She started to walk away.

"Wait!" Burke called after her. "When are we going?"

"Next week!" She called.

Burke stormed up to his room, slamming the door behind him. His fists balled, fingernails digging into his palm. He looked around, his face growing more and more red with anger and hatred. Looking towards his dirt-smudged walls, Burke wrinkled his face and lunged out. His shoeless heel went into the wall, making a large dent where his foot still stuck. Burke kicked it again, this time he flung his heel out sideways, like a karate kick. When he was finally calming down, Burke stopped to look at the damage. He had left a small crater in the wall, with a chunk of wall that still flapped over. Plaster dust stuck in his carpet and to the bottom of his sock. Burke ignored the mess, grabbed a roll of duct tape and patched it up. He didn't feel like getting into any other trouble with his mom, so he thought he might as well try to fix it. When he stepped back to take a look at his handiwork, the wall looked worse than before. Gray duct tape dangled in awkward positions, mostly sticking to itself more than to the wall.

Burke sighed, *Oh well. Joke's on them if they can't sell the house.* He thought. He went to his desk, powered up his computer and logged into his favorite game and entered the chat room. Burke only saw one other person in the room. He was sitting on the only couch, facing one of the huge windows. Today, the scenery was a tropical beach, with crashing waves and white sparkling sand. There were palm trees and coconuts growing around the deserted island.

"Ahem." Burke cleared his throat. The figure sitting on the couch turned to face him. It was Damien. Even in a crowd of hundreds of players, Damien would be the easiest to spot. His avatar had distinct features and always wore the brightest and coolest clothes. His virtual wardrobe had hundreds of different outfits in it, from questionable speedos to full-length winter parkas. Burke had always been a little jealous of Damien's inventory.

"Hey," Damien finally said.

"Hi. Sorry, didn't mean to interrupt." Burke crossed around the room and stopped at the window, taking in the scenery.

"Nah, you're fine." Damien's character nodded at Burke.

"How about a little spar. One on one?" Burke asked with a wide grin.

"Why not?" Damien got up from the couch and his character disappeared as he logged into the main game hub. Burke followed.

Chapter 3

It was late afternoon, Burke sat on the couch and returned to staring at the blank wall where the TV used to be.

"Burke!" His mother cried. "I don't want to have to tell you again, go pack your room!"

"Mom! I am not moving! You and Dad and Sally can go wherever you want, but I am staying right here."

"Burke, if you don't pack your stuff we will just leave it all behind, including your gaming things!"

"Fine!" Burke said as he rolled his eyes. He got up, stormed up to his room, and started furiously shoving all his possessions into the empty cardboard boxes. Most of Burke's belongings were gaming manuals, candy bar wrappers, old crumpled homework, empty plastic water bottles, laptops, games and dirty clothes. He tossed his unmatched socks, crumpled T-shirts, and stiff shorts into the boxes. When Burke packed his laptops, he carefully placed them into the box, making sure there was plenty of toilet paper wrapped around to protect them. He didn't appreciate any other things he owned, except for his electronics.

In only a few hours he was finished with his packing. Burke slid all his moving boxes down the stairs, watching them bump down each step. They flipped and tumbled at the bottom of the landing, and Burke could hear things breaking and bumping around in the boxes. *Oh, I'll just blame that on Sally. She's so careless!* Burke thought as returned to his place on the couch. He crossed his arms and sighed, slumping further into the sofa. *I can't believe we're actually moving*, he thought to himself. *Or is this just a dream?* He pinched his arm to make sure he was awake. *Is it even possible for someone to move in two days?* He sighed. *They're crazy!* He thought.

"Hey kid, we gotta move this couch, you gotta get up."

Burke looked up at the two men. They stood over him, arms crossed, both wearing gray tank tops that were probably once white. One of the men chewed on the end of a toothpick while the other picked his nails with boredom. "We're moving this into the truck, get up."

Burke got up and watched the movers heave the well-worn couch into the truck. They pulled down the heavy metal door and latched it with a final thump. The engine sputtered a few times and then took off. Burke watched as the truck pulled away, leaving him in a cloud of diesel.

They had been driving for over an hour now. Sally was softly snoring, curled up in the corner of the car. However, Burke was still staring at his phone. "Mom!" He whined, "I don't have any service!"

She held out her hand. "Give me your phone. When we get to the new house you won't even need this anymore. There isn't a cell tower within miles of the new house."

"No!" he retorted, "I'm not giving up anything else."

The scenery soon changed. Street lights were replaced by blossoming trees, and colorful leaves crunched under their tires on the winding road. As the day grew dim, Burke noticed stars in the sky, something he would have never seen in the city. As they continued on their drive, the stars grew brighter as the sun dipped below a ridge. When the sun had totally disappeared, Burke could see the entire Milky Way, shining brighter than he had ever seen before.

△ △ △

The house was eerie at night, with only a few solar-powered lights leading up the stairs to the front door. Burke's mom had been right about one thing: The house *was* huge. Burke stared up at the mahogany double doors. Each door had a silver knocker the size of Burke's fist. There were even pillars and a fountain in the front driveway.

Burke tried not to look deep into the woods that surrounded him. He ran straight to the house, his phone flashlight bouncing along with him.

"Burke!" his mom called after him. "You forgot your backpack! Come and get it!"

"Um, no thanks! I'll get it in the morning." He called to her without looking back. "I am not spending any more time around here in the dark." He said quietly to himself, once again eying the wooded pathways and roads.

Chapter 4

The computer powered on and automatically opened up his game center. Burke scrolled through notifications, chats, and new updates before he finally logged on to his main chat group. He could already see all of his virtual friends in the chat room, their animated characters wandering around the home base, awaiting his instruction. Burke had designed and furnished the chat room. He envisioned a modern theme with floor to ceiling windows that looked out into a different animated setting and place every day. Burke had left the furniture minimal, and any that he purchased was the most expensive and top quality. He hadn't spent any money for three months, just so he could buy the latest edition of the furnishings in their virtual living room.

After showing his leadership skills and dedication, Burke had been appointed the leader of his "clan" and took his role very seriously. He had led his team through numerous battles and skill training sessions. They were currently ranked 36 out of 434 teams. Over the gaming world, this made Burke well known and somewhat popular. However, in the real world, if Burke were to disappear, he wondered if it would even be noticed.

"Burke!" All his gamer friends cheered as he joined the server, their characters gathering around him.

"Hey, guys!" He replied with their same enthusiasm.

"What are we playing today?" Billy asked as he materialized in the corner.

"Zombie Creatures Volume 2! It's the undead monkeys versus us. If we beat this level, I'll be able to reach level 26!" Damien answered over the headset.

"Yeah, same here," Anthony added.

"Burke, you're on level 34. How'd you beat the monkeys?" Billy asked.

"Guys, the monkeys can be controlled by any player that has reached over level 27, so I have no idea how these ones are gonna attack. They have a different strategy every time. But here's the plan. We hide behind the Dungeon and sneak up on the monkeys' base, begin fire, and we win!"

"You make it sound so easy," Kyle, another team member, complained.

"Wait! Did you guys hear that?" Billy asked, sounding anxious. "It sounded like breathing. Kind of like my uncle's breathing, and he's got sleep apnea. Do you think we're getting hacked again?"

"C'mon Billy." Everyone groaned in annoyance.

"Don't be so paranoid dude." Damien laughed at him. "Just because we got hacked one time doesn't mean it's gonna happen again. Plus, we got a securer server now."

"Ok never mind, it was nothing," Billy said, still sounding unsure.

"Ok then," Kyle interrupted the conversation. "Are we done now?"

"Yeah, let's head out." Anthony chimed in, and the team made their way to the battlefield.

Three hours passed and Burke still hadn't moved an inch, except for the furious flicking of his fingers as he shot rabid zombies and chased after flying monkeys. He could feel aching in his wrists, which he had self-diagnosed to be premature carpal tunnel. Burke ignored the throbbing pains shooting through his hands and continued to press the buttons on his controller repeatedly. Burke had many self-diagnoses. He found he was nearsighted, but noticed he could correct it by squinting really hard. Rapidly blinking and squinting his bloodshot eyes, Burke tried to stay awake. In the corner of the screen, he watched an undead monkey land in front of him. He cocked his gun and gazed through the scope. The television screen automatically switched views, and the monkey now looked huge. Burke shifted his finger to the shoot button. *If I can just hit him right in the head he'll be done in one blow,* he thought to himself.

"Burke!" Multiple people shouted over the headset at once. "Behind you!" Damien cried, his voice cracking with fear as he shouted. Burke whipped around, spiraling the thumb joystick. Another flying monkey had landed behind him with its gun raised. Thinking quick, Burke switched his weapon to a short blade. He didn't know if his knife handling skills would finally pay off, but it was worth a shot.

"Ha! You think you're going to do any damage with that tiny thing?" The flying monkey crackled over the headset.

"Hey! How'd he do that?" Anthony exclaimed. "This is a private chat!"

"I told you there were hackers!" Billy exclaimed triumphantly.

"Yeah, we were too late to hear your 'master plan' though." The monkey said.

"But we'll finish this anyway! Fair and square," his teammate sneered.

"Uh, technically--" Billy began.

"Shut up, Billy!" Damien cut him off mid-sentence.

"Watch and learn, fellas" Burke grinned.

He raised his blade and stole a glance toward the other monkey. Carefully, he watched both monkeys close in on him. With a quick flick of his wrist, he threw the knife at the creature. It seemed to spiral in slow motion and hit the monkey square in the chest. The monkey disintegrated into a pile of dust and disappeared. The second one was so surprised, Burke heard him gasp over the headset.

"Maybe hacking us wasn't such a good idea," Burke taunted as he blew a hole right through the monkey's skull.

"Not too bad of a trick." The hacker said as he, too, disintegrated into a pile of dust. "It's pretty good for beginner's luck."

"Beginner's luck?" Burke scoffed. "I'm definitely not a beginner!"

"Yeah whatever, what level are you on, kid?" the hacker asked. He respawned and now his character stood in front of Burke. The hacker's character was tall and pale, with customized tattoos running down his arms. Burke gave him a once-over, with a look of disgust.

"34," Burke said, trying to sound cool.

"Yeah, like I said, beginner's luck."

"Ok fine, what level are you on?"

"39" The voice replied.

"Yeah right." Burke scoffed at him, "Only three people in the world have beaten level thirty-five and I know all of them *personally*. There's no way you beat it."

"I never said you had to believe me."

Burke clenched his jaw, taking slow, deep breaths. *Who does this guy think he is?* Burke thought. "Prove it." he finally blurted, "Prove that you beat level 35. Show me the Sword of Dardious."

The sword of Dardious was the magical sword many avid gamers hoped to obtain. Only those who beat level 35 automatically won the weapon.

"Sure thing, kid." The hacker pulled a silver shimmering sword out of his inventory and held it out in front of Burke.

"Whoa!" Kyle interrupted.

"I have never seen that in person before!" Billy said in admiration.

"Like it?" He taunted Burke, waving it before his face.

"Since you're such a good hacker, you probably hacked your inventory just to get the sword," Burke said defiantly.

"Aww," The hacker cooed, "You think I'm a good hacker?"

"No, that's not what I meant!" Burke gritted his teeth. This guy was really starting to get on his nerves.

"It's what you *said*." The hacker laughed at Burke.

"Forget I said anything at all. How'd you get the sword, then?" Despite the attitude of the hacker, Burke was still intrigued.

"And why should I tell you?"

"Fine. Here's the deal. I will teach you how to knife throw and you will teach me to beat level 35."

"I don't need to learn how to knife throw, kid." The hacker retorted. "Why don't you go teach your own little friends." He said with a chuckle at his own joke.

"Well, this is kinda boring now. Logging off." Damien announced.

"Ya, same here," Kyle said. The rest of Burke's team members logged off the chat and Burke was left alone with the hacker.

"Look, I just want to get past level 35. What can I do?" Burke had resorted to pleading.

"Fine!" The hacker had lost his cool, "I can't deal with you little kids." He mumbled under his breath. "Transfer fifty bitcoins to me and I'll help you. But if you don't have the money, then you'll have to find someone else."

"Ok! I got it!" Burke said excitedly. He had been saving up all of his allowance money for over a month to buy the latest gaming software, but this was better. "I'm Burke, by the way."

"You can call me Triton." The hacker replied.

Chapter 5

"Can you get off the internet already?" Burke called down the stairs to his parents.

"We are doing important work stuff. Go play outside, or at least do something active! You don't need it anyway." His mom shouted back.

"Why don't you go play outside! You're the one who loves the nature." Burke retorted.

"Burke!" She was getting annoyed, "stop complaining or you won't be able to use it at all."

"It's not my fault you had to get the slowest connection so only one person could use it at a time!" He shouted back, straining his voice with annoyance.

Burke sat in his empty room, looking around at his still packed moving boxes. It was a month since the move, and he was still in denial about it. He didn't want to admit it was permanent. *There's still a chance we could move back.* Burke would think to himself every day. He rolled onto his bed, which was really just a mattress on the floor. He was still lacking a bed frame and didn't care to put his old one together. Burke threw his blankets on the ground, hunting for his laptop in the bed sheets. He would often fall asleep with the computer resting on his chest and wouldn't be able to find it in the mornings. This was how Burke found out he had restless leg syndrome. He would sometimes find the laptop kicked to the ground or fully splayed out at the foot of his bed. This was another self-diagnosis, which Burke had confirmed with WebMD.

"Are you done yet?" Burke called out again. He yawned. *Here comes my narcolepsy.* "If you don't hurry, I'll fall asleep."

"Fine, I'm done now, but you only have ten minutes," his mom yelled up the stairs, ignoring his last comment.

"Yes!" He pumped his fist and logged on. Opening up his game center, he noticed one new notification. It was a chat request from Triton. "Save phone number and don't ever share it. Delete message when done." Under the message was Triton's phone number. Burke fumbled around for his own phone in his bed sheets, hoping it was near where his laptop had been. He groaned, remembering he had left it on the counter downstairs. Burke launched out of bed, slipping on the wood floor in his socks as he raced down the stairs taking two steps at a time. He flew past his parents in their bedroom, looking sideways at them as they chatted quietly. Burke grabbed his phone off the counter, making his way back upstairs, with less of a rush this time. *That's weird.* He thought as he approached his parents. *They hardly ever have real conversations.* Burke stopped at their door, eavesdropping on them.

"I wish Burke would get off of that computer," his mom said to his dad. "He can't spend his whole life playing video games and watching YouTube." She sighed and looked out the window into their huge yard. "Remember when we were kids? This place would have been so fun for us. We would run through the sprinklers, jump in the leaf piles and explore nature." She shook her head at the thought of her two kids, cooped up in their rooms probably just playing on their iPads.

"Don't worry too much. This will be taken care of by the new year." They both smiled at each other.

What was that about? Burke forgot about Triton for a minute. He was too focused on his parents' conversation.

Oh no! They're going to send me away to some brainwashed boarding school! And they're probably going to sell my Xbox! He worried. *They can't do this!* Burke's thoughts quickly switched from worry to anger as he stomped back to his room.

Chapter 6

Burke kicked at the ground, scattering leaves and dust into the air. He sighed and leaned against a tree. I didn't even get my full ten minutes on the internet! He thought. *At least I can talk to Triton. I guess he's better than this nature stuff*, Burke thought to himself as he looked around. He walked away from the back door and toward a path into the woods. He looked up and scowled at the birds singing in the trees. When he kicked the soil again, his foot hit against something hard. "Ow!" He cried. "Stupid rock." He picked it up and threw it as hard as he could into the forest. Burke watched the rock fall through the trees, crashing into dry leaves and stick branches.

He kept walking, thinking about how much he hated the last few months in this house. "Oh let's just pack up and move now." Burke imitated his mother in a high-pitched voice. *How could they keep a secret like that from me? What else are they hiding?* Burke thought. He suddenly remembered the strange conversation that he had overheard. Everything was starting to add up now. By next year it would be a new semester, they weren't going on any winter vacations and he had heard his mom on the phone with his principal. *I knew it. They're sending me to boarding school.* Burke clenched his fists, thinking about all the times they had kept secrets from him.

Burke had made it to the edge of the woods. He looked behind him towards his house in the distance. He could see the perfectly cut green grass. As he looked, the sprinklers came on and the whole image looked so normal. However, where he stood the ground was covered in dry dirt and fallen leaves. This area was definitely forgotten by the gardeners and everyone else. As his rants turned into grumbles, he sauntered down an overgrown path and came to a row of barn-sized sheds. He had noticed them before but never cared to check them out.

The sheds were completely made out of metal and had big wide doors with heavy padlocks on them. The locks looked rusted and old as they dangled towards the ground. Burke frowned, why were these locks so old looking if the house had just been built? He shrugged and strode over to the first shed. The padlock hung open on the door, which wasn't closed all the way. He looked inside. A small chain hung from the ceiling, slowly swaying back and forth. He was terrified of the dark. Burke pulled down on the chain and a light right above him lit up the room. He shivered, fear tying his stomach in knots. Old crates in the corner of the room looked like a hunched person, and bugs scurrying around the floor made creepy scraping sounds. Burke grimaced and looked from side to side, eyeing the dark corners of the room where the dim light couldn't reach. He finally found the strength to move and ran out of the shed as fast as he could, slamming the door behind him. Adrenaline coursed through his blood and he vowed to never look in that shed again. In a full sprint, Burke didn't take his eyes off the house. *There won't be any monsters or ghosts there.* Burke thought.

As he got farther away from the shed, his thoughts turned back to his parents. Burke recalled all the weird things they had been up to. *Maybe they aren't who they say they are! They made us move last minute and have been having suspicious conversations about me and Sally.* Burke thought about the internet speed. *Why did they get such a slow connection when they could have easily gotten a better one?*

He went through the house and to the office. The router sat under the desk, cords and wires running all over the place. Burke bent down, trying to get a better look at the box. "T-50X1000?" Burke said aloud to himself. "That can't be right." He texted Triton. *This is the fastest router on the market, right?* He asked him.

Ya, how'd you get one? Triton replied within seconds. *Those are super rare... and expensive! And I mean EXPENSIVE.* Triton emphasized the last word in all caps.

How many devices can run on it at once?

Up to 20 with no issue. Why?

Just curious. Is it possible for it to be slow with only one device? Burke asked.

No way! Those things are like military grade. Triton exaggerated.

Ok, so the only way for it to be slow is if there are more than 20 devices on it? Burke questioned

Exactly. Triton replied.

Thanks for the help. Burke texted back.

No prob. Bye!

How is this possible? Burke thought. *The WiFi is slow with only one device.*

"Sally!" Burke called out the office door.

"What?"

"Have you been using the WiFi?" he asked.

"Nope." She came into the room. "Why?"

"It's nothing, the connection is just super slow. Which is kinda impossible, considering the speed this thing should have," Burke said to Sally with an "I know more than you" voice.

"Ya, whatever, Burke. Mom and Dad have been using it a lot though, maybe it's them."

"Maybe," Burke said, unconvinced.

△ △ △

Burke stared out his bedroom window. He watched the stars flicker in the pitch black sky. He sighed and slumped down into his bed. *Why does it have to be me?* Burke thought. *Why am I the one who has to move out to the middle of nowhere?*

Burke propped his head on top of his arms, resting against his headboard. He sat still for a moment, not thinking of anything, just staring at his blank wall. He was startled by a soft sputter of a car engine. Burke quickly sat up and peered out the window again. He saw a car pull out of the driveway.

Chapter 7

Burke watched the family SUV pull out of the driveway at a crawl. The headlights were off, and he could make out the silhouettes of his parents in the front seats, dressed all in black.

Where are they going? Burke thought. Was this the secret they were hiding from him? *Maybe they're getting sick of these woods too? Are they headed to the city?* Burke watched a little longer as they turned towards the direction of town. He leaped out of bed with a glimmer of hope. If his parents also hated this nature, maybe they could move back home.

Burke snuck out of the house and crept around to the back, searching for his bike in the dim moonlight. He grabbed the handles and finally pulled it out from the bush where it had been stuck. Burke strapped on his helmet and sped down the street after them.

He followed them for a half hour until they finally got to town. His parents took back streets and alleyways, and he tagged along, but not too close, making sure he wasn't seen. He finally came to a stop about a block away from where his parents had parked. He hopped off his bike and tiptoed up the street, trying to stay out of the dim light coming from street lamps. Burke had never been to this side of town. He shivered in the cold, looking around at the desolate industrial buildings. When he reached the place where his parents' car was parked, all he could see was a gray cement, rectangular building. Burke crept around the SUV and crouched near the tire, watching his parents at the door. They pulled out a badge and swiped it across a sensor. *How'd they get that?* Burke wondered. The door hissed open and both his parents stepped inside.

Burke waited a few seconds, making sure his parents were gone and then crept closer to the building. He saw something on a plaque near the door. The plaque didn't have the name of the building or a description, there was just a short quote: "Back to the beginning." Confused, Burke whipped out his phone and looked up the phrase. He spent almost ten minutes scrolling through movies and songs, but couldn't find anything related to the town. He had one last idea. He texted Triton.

Triton can find anything, Burke reassured himself when he hadn't texted back for over ten minutes.

When Triton finally returned the text, all he said was, *Do you think I'm an amateur?*

Burke was confused, *What?*

No need to send your location. I can hack your phone. I know where you are.

I didn't send my location. That's what I'm trying to figure out.

Triton replied. *Well, I already know.*

Triton sent one last text: *That quote matches a plaque on the building that's the same as your current GPS location, this was too easy. It looks like this building was used for some sort of electrical engineering back in the day but it's abandoned now.*

Is that it? Burke asked.

Of course it is! There's nothing else. Like I said, I'm no amateur... I'm the best.

Burke was still persistent, *Are you sure? There has to be something else! You must have overlooked something!*

Triton didn't reply.

Burke returned his attention the building just in time to hear the door hiss open again. He fled to the nearest hiding spot behind the car. Burke could hear voices from the doorway. He slowly looked up through the car windows and caught a glimpse of another person walking beside his parents. Burke watched the three carry large boxes toward the car.

"I'll get the door," he heard one of them say. Burke gulped and awkwardly tried to scooch around the car so no one would see him.

Burke cautiously stood, trying to get a view of them as they loaded boxes into the trunk. In the last second, he accidentally bumped his head on the driver's side door. With a loud siren, the car alarm started to blare, and Burke leaped away, adrenaline coursing through his blood. Bounding around the car and leaping across the sidewalk, Burke managed to find his bike lying in some bushes. He swung his legs over and pumped as hard as he could, his legs burning from exertion. He looked behind him and saw his mom slamming the car door. Burke stood up on his bike pedaling harder and faster than before.

"Hey! Get back here!" Burke recognized that familiar voice. His dad. Burke 's heart stopped and his stomach dropped. *If I can just get away, they still don't know it's me.* He didn't stop to look back, just kept going, full speed.

"Get back here! I know it's you, Burke!" The same voice said from behind him. His dad was straining for breath and every time he took a step towards Burke, another painful wheeze would erupt from his lungs.

Burke tried his hardest to pull away from the chase, but soon, he too was wheezing. He felt a sudden jolt and was tossed up and over his handlebars, suspended in the air for a moment. Then, everything came crashing towards him, the black asphalt, the cold, concrete ground. With the great impact, Burke groaned and rolled onto his back. Out of the corner of his eye, he could see the rock that his bike had been flipped over. Burke curled into a fetal position, awaiting his father's wrath.

"Burke?" His father came towering over him.

"Hi, Dad," Burke replied sheepishly.

"What the heck are you doing here?"

"Sorry, I just wanted to see what you and mom were doing here."

"We had work to attend to." His dad replied as another figure appeared over Burke.

"Get up off the ground. It's filthy." Burke's mother added as she crossed her arms, looking at him as if he was purposely lying on the ground with cuts and bruises.

Burke stood, wobbling slightly. He looked over at his bike, its tires still spinning while it lay sideways in the street. He walked over and picked it up, examining the frame.

"So, explain yourself, Burke." His mother said.

Burke panicked, he couldn't think of anything.

"Well, I thought you were going for ice cream so I followed you here." He said under his breath.

"What was that?" His father intervened.

"I thought you were getting ice cream?" Even to Burke it sounded weak.

They laughed at him. "Well, we were just getting some fresh air." Burke's mom said. "But if you want ice cream go ahead! We'll be heading home now." Burke's mom said and made her way back to the car.

"You can bike home, Burke." His father said.

△ △ △

On the way home, Burke swerved down the empty road, his bike making odd sounds as he pedaled. It seemed a little lopsided from his crash. *There's something weird about that building.* Burke thought. *Why were they putting stuff in the car? And that saying, back to the beginning, what's that supposed to mean?* Burke shook his head in frustration. This was too creepy.

Chapter 8

It had been weeks since the late night spying incident, and Burke had mostly tried to avoid his parents. The days had gone by and no one mentioned anything about that night. Burke didn't speak much to his parents anymore, and they both seemed overly nice and less parent like. Sally was totally oblivious to the awkward tension between Burke and his parents.

△ △ △

Burke tore open the package, expecting the sleek black case of his new headphones, but instead there was only cleaning supplies. He sighed and sat back on his heels.

"Mom!" Burke called up the stairs.

"What?" She replied.

"There's a package for you!" He shouted again.

"What is it?" she yelled back.

Burke riffled through the package and dumped its contents onto the floor. "Dishwashing gloves, some spray stuff, and toilet paper..." Burke trailed off as something else caught his eye. He picked it up and examined it.

"Mom!" he called out again, "did you order a taser?" Burke put the weapon back down, not wanting to accidentally set it off. She didn't reply. Burke gulped. He pushed the contents of the box away from him and stood up to go outside. Burke pushed open the door and sat on the top step. He ran his finger along a crack beside him, trying to push away the fear that was slowly creeping up inside him.

He pulled out his phone, a new text message alert appeared on his screen. It was from Triton. "Wanna play Zombies?" It read. Burke checked the date. The message was from two days ago. *Why didn't I see this earlier?* He thought to himself. Burke shrugged and texted Triton back, *Sorry I must have just gotten your text. I was probably outta range.*

He sent the message and leaned back against the steps. Almost instantly, his phone chimed and a new message from Triton popped up.

No problem. What are you doing?

Burke looked at his phone and was puzzled. He reread the message. *This is weird,* he thought to himself. *Triton never makes small talk. Everyone has been acting so strange lately.*

Burke remembered the taser again. He decided to ask Triton about it.

Can I ask you something? Burke texted.

Triton replied with a question mark.

What do you know about tasers? Burke sent.

A lot. Why? Triton asked.

Burke called Triton. Maybe it would be easier explaining over the phone. However, Triton declined immediately.

Can't talk now, just text. Triton wrote.

So weird! Burke thought again.

Triton wouldn't usually say any of this. Burke shrugged. *People change I guess*, he thought to himself and resumed texting his friend.

Triton's final answer after hearing the whole story was, *Don't worry about it, Burke. It's pretty normal that your mom would buy a taser.*

Burke shook his head at this. This was the worst advice Triton had ever given him. Even worse was that Triton really had changed. He never called Burke by his real name, usually coming up with a different stupid nickname every day.

Burke quickly stood up, "I can't take this place anymore!" He yelled out into dark nothingness. His words echoed back to him and Burke groaned. He whacked at the dirt on his shoes with a look of disgust. he hated the trees and hated the birds. He especially hated the dust. Burke kicked some leaves out of his way and headed out onto the trail, not having a specific destination.

He walked aimlessly through the woods, dragging his feet through the dry leaves and staring down the squirrels in the trees. Finally he made his way back to the trail and followed it further. Burke looked up from the ground and found himself back at the sheds.

"I better get outta here." Burke thought to himself as he looked up at the dark sky and remembered his first encounter with these sheds. However, as he turned, he noticed something different about the first shed. Burke took and few steps closer. The old rusty locks were replaced with shiny new ones, still unlocked. Instead of checking out the first shed he had seen before, Burke peeked into the other two.

The second shed was filled with rows and rows of canned foods, locked behind metal bars.

"What is this all for?" Burke whispered to himself. "Why do we need so much food? Maybe they're going on that extreme survivalist show?" Burke said aloud as he peered around in the dimly lit space.

I guess that would be kinda cool, he thought.

Burke walked around the outside of the third shed and carefully opened this door. This shed was empty. He stepped inside and walked around slowly, running his hand along the wall. Burke noticed an additional door in the corner, he approached the door, and turned the knob, entering into a brightly lit hallway. Burke stopped for a moment. *What is this place?* he thought to himself.

The hallway was gray and empty, with the feel of a sterile place like a hospital. When he reached the end of the hallway, he found himself in another room. This one was smaller and was empty, except for a single red button on top of a pedestal. It was encased in a clear glass box. *I probably shouldn't press it*, Burke thought. *But if I don't, I'll never know what it's for.* He lifted the glass cover and pressed the button.

Some sort of screen popped up in front of him. He held out his hand and tried to touch it, but his hand went right through and touched the cold wall on the other side. *Is this a hologram?* Burke walked around the screen to make sure it wasn't just a projection on the wall. The hologram looked like a computer screen, except it didn't seem to have any controls. Burke held up his hand and swiped through the air, pretending he was in a sci-fi movie. The hologram disappeared for a moment, but then reappeared, this time showing a different image.

"Woah!" Burke said. "That actually worked!"

Burke returned his attention to the hologram. It looked like some kind of lock page, one that would be on a computer. There was a small rectangular box in the middle with a flashing cursor and the word "password" underneath. Burke had gotten this far, but he didn't think he would be lucky enough to guess the password.

Chapter 9

Burke heard a loud thump from outside the room. He backed up to the farthest wall, his heart pounding. A door shaped section of the wall morphed into a hole. Burke pressed his body into a corner of the room, trying to steady his breath. He could hear his heart beating so loud, he was sure whoever was standing on the other side of the hole could hear it too. Burke watched as a foot stepped into the room. He kept his eyes locked on the floor and finally could make out the whole shape of a person in his peripheral vision. Burke squeezed his eyes shut, hoping he could just disappear.

Maybe I've found some secret military base and they're coming after me! Burke's imagination raced with crazy scenarios. *They're gonna capture me and put me in jail and not tell my family! And I'll live-*

"Oh, you're here!" Burke's thoughts were interrupted by a familiar voice. He slowly looked up to see his dad standing near the wall opening. The morphing door closed behind the him. Burke still stood in the corner, not moving. "Well, this will have to quicken our plans, but that's fine I guess," his dad finally said.

Burke looked up, confused. "What plans?" he managed to say.

"Well, let me start from the beginning." Burke's dad said and cleared his throat. "When we were living in the old house, we realized how much you and Sally would *always* be on the screens. So, we decided to move into the woods so you could experience the nature. But, once we saw the great progress, we came up with a way for the whole country to experience this too!"

Burke was just confused, "Why would you do that? There are people in the world who *depend* on the internet."

His dad laughed, "Like your hacker friend, Triton?"

"Yeah," Burke said. "But how do you know about him?"

Burke's dad stuck out his hand, "Nice to meet you, Burke. I'm Triton."

"No." Burke said and took a step back. "Not possible. Was it this whole time?"

"Well, no. Not exactly. I'm also a hacker, and when I hacked your phone and found out you were getting suspicious, I decided to handle things myself."

Burke's eyes widened. "What did you do to Triton?"

"Simple, I paid him two thousand dollars and he gladly moved to Mexico. Never to be seen again." His dad smiled at the end of this.

"No, this is crazy. This is a joke, right?" Burke shook his head.

"No, sorry, son. But since you know the plan now, I'll have to set things off early." He fished a walkie-talkie of his pocket and spoke into it. A moment later, Burke's mom showed up with Sally at her side. She didn't acknowledge Burke.

His mom strode across the room and swiped up in the air. The hologram came up with the same password page. Burke carefully watched as she typed in the password. He automatically memorized the eight-digit string of numbers. Burke's mom pulled up another page after the lock screen. It looked like a blueprint of the town. It showed their house marked with a red dot and another red dot on the building Burke's parents had been to a few weeks back. All of the other few houses in the town were marked with yellow dots, and the rundown industrial buildings marked with blue ones.

Burke's mom tapped in the air and the image zoomed in on their property.

"Ready?" Burke's mom looked back at her husband. He gave a slight nod and she flicked the air. Burke heard the sound of sliding deadbolts and latching locks.

"What's happening?" Burke's eyes darted back and forth between his parents.

"We'll explain later," his dad said as he opened an invisible door Burke hadn't seen.

"No!" Burke pushed his dad away. "Why are we here? Why did you lock the doors? Where does this door lead?" Burke blabbered with questions.

His mother calmly walked through the door. "C'mon Burke. Don't be like this." She grabbed his hand and dragged him through the door.

"Let me go!" He struggled to fight her off but her grip tightened.

She looked toward her husband and they both burst out in laughter. "No time for jokes Burke, we have to hurry."

"Hurry for what?" He tried to pull away again. Burke's dad pushed in front of the two of them and made his way to the center of the room. Burke's mom gave one last tug and he tumbled into the room after her. His mom finally let go of him as she also made her way to the center of the room. Burke looked around and saw a huge table with five 60" monitor screens. It looked like a control room you would find in a space station or an evil villain's secret hideout. There was another big hologram in this room with strings of code running along it as Burke's dad typed at the computers. His dad sat in a leather rolling chair and pushed himself back and forth among the monitors.

"What is this place?" Burke crossed his arms. "Tell me what's going on!"

"Burke, we were going to explain everything in the future, but you're the one who had to go snooping around. Now you've basically ruined our plans. So be quiet and we'll explain later." His mother glared at him as she said this.

"And done!" Burke's dad stood up and watched all the monitors power down one by one. Then, the lights went out and everything turned black.

"What did you do?!" Burke fumbled around in the dark.

"Hold on one sec." The lights came back on and Burke looked around. His mother stood by a small backup battery-powered generator and Sally stood at her side holding her hand. Burke's dad still sat in his chair with a grin on his face.

"What did you just do?" Burke asked again. "Why is all of this here? Why do you guys have a secret underground base? Why do you have a warehouse of canned food, and why don't you ever tell me anything!?"

"Burke, just trust us, you'll understand when you're older."

"Trust you?!" Burke found himself at a loss for words. "How do you expect me to trust you while this is happening?" Burke was flabbergasted.

"And what exactly do you think is happening?" His mother cocked her head like a dog.

"You're, um, you're evil!" Burke was caught off guard by this question.

"No, Burke!" His mother sweetly said, "We are saving mankind. And you're helping!"

"No! I will not be part of your evil schemes!" Burke was terrified inside.

Sally still stood by her mom's side. She was starting to let go of her hand. "Are you really evil mommy?" She asked, close to tears.

"No sweetie, Burke is making it up."

"C'mon Sally, you can't trust them. Come over here."

Sally looked back and forth from her parents to Burke. She burst out in tears, sobbing and shaking.

"Oh, I'm sorry hon, we didn't mean to scare you." Burke's mother reached out to Sally but she ran to the farthest corner of the room, away from both parents and from Burke.

"Ok Burke, it's us versus you. Now tell me, who do you think will win?"

Burke was just confused now. "Is this some sort of game?"

"Oh no!" Burke's mother laughed. "We're way past that, sweetie. This is war." She started pacing the room. "Basically, we shut down all of the main power stations across America so no one has any electricity. Imagine, families across America, camping and sitting around their campfires." She chuckled and sat in the leather chair, spinning in circles. "Obviously we can use electricity responsibly, but the rest of the world will have to learn. We have our solar panels and are very prepared. I assume you saw the stock of food?" She pushed herself around the room, happy and giggly like a child.

"Why would you do this?" Burke looked at both of his parents. "Are you like terrorists or something?" Burke started backing up. He didn't want to be near them.

"No of course not! We just want families to get the chance to experience nature. They shouldn't always be on their phones and computers, wasting their lives."

"You don't have to cause chaos to the rest of the country. Do you even realize what people will do if they can't get around with cars, or buy food, or use their Xboxes?" Burke's eyes widened. He just realized that he wouldn't ever be able to play video games.

"Don't make this about yourself, Burke. There are probably people being killed out there for food and money." Burke's mom reasoned.

"Yeah, because of you!" Burke shouted at her.

"Well, that's beside the point." She flicked her hair with pride.

"I guess we *do* have some explaining to do." Burke's dad said, looking over to his mom. "The internet was always slow because of these monitors and holograms here. We ordered all the food and stocked up because who knows how long we'll be here? And those late night outings, well, we were just figuring out the logistics of our little plan."

△ △ △

Burke had been sitting in the corner with Sally for what seemed like hours. His parents conspired with each other in the opposite corner.

What is happening? Burke was still in shock. *They are so crazy. I just need to get out of this room!* He was starting to feel stir crazy and claustrophobic. *If only I could get access to the computer, I could unlock the door.*

"Mom!" He jumped up. "How long are we gonna be here?"

His mother looked towards him. "So you're being nice now?"

"I had a change of heart. I realized that you and Dad were right. It was the only thing you could do. In fact, you saved the world!" Burke lied so well he even believed himself.

"Oh, I'm glad you could see that, honey." She smiled wide with her perfect white teeth. "Well, a dear friend of your father's and mine who helped us with our little project will come by and get us when things settle down."

"And how soon will that be?" Burke questioned.

"Soon enough." Burke's father replied. He looked down at his watch. "It's getting late. You kids better get ready for bed." Burke's father strolled over to a computer and typed in a command. Another door appeared across the room. Burke followed his family through this one and stepped into the room.

"Here is the bathroom!" Burke's dad flung his arm around in a wide gesture. The bathroom was quite large, there were two sinks, a separate door that went to the toilet, and a huge shower. On the bare side of the bathroom, there were three more doors. Burke peeked through all the doors. They each were replicas of their bedrooms at the house. Burke found his and locked himself in the room. Finally, he had a plan.

△ △ △

At midnight, Burke crept out of his room. He tiptoed through the bathroom and made his way to the control center door. It slowly opened without a sound and Burke looked around inside. The lights on the monitor power buttons blinked in the darkness. Still tiptoeing, he started to make his way to the computers. The leather chair faced away from him and Burke reached out to pull it toward him. The chair suddenly spun around and Burke could make out the figure of a person sitting with their arms crossed. He screamed and jumped back, falling on the floor.

This was such a mistake! Burke tried to push himself backward but he smacked the back of his head on the desk and fell to the ground again.

When he woke up, all the lights were on in the room and Burke's father stood over him.

"Hey! Didn't mean to scare you." He chuckled.

"I was just, umm, I couldn't sleep." Burke stammered.

"Me too." His father replied. "That's why I was sitting in the chair."

"Oh right." Burke now recalled what had happened.

"You scream like a girl." His dad burst out into laughter.

Burke just stared at him, his brow furrowed. "So how did you become Triton?" Burke tried to casually change the subject.

"Funny story actually. After I hacked your phone, I forwarded all your texts to myself. So while you were chatting away with your friend, I was also keeping an eye out. I saw you starting to get close to the truth, that night you followed us to our headquarters. So I decided to take matters into my own hands." His dad nodded at his own genius plan.

"Are you telling the truth? Is Triton really in Mexico? Is he ok?" Burke asked.

"I'm telling the truth, Burke. Why would I make this up anyway? I told him to move out of the country, and he gladly did. You really need to find some *real* friends, Burke. I mean loyal ones." His dad smirked at him.

Burke rolled his eyes, once again changing the subject. "I think I understand your plan now. I can see where you have a point." Burke coolly lied. His *own* plan was finally taking action. "I'm gonna go to bed now." Burke got up and turned away.

"Night son. And thanks for supporting your mother and me, I'm glad that you understand."

Burke cleared his throat. "Of course!" he lied again. *Wow.* Burke was almost impressed. *They really are crazy.* He made his way back to his bed. *My plan will just have to wait until tomorrow night.* However, it wasn't until after a few weeks that Burke could finally carry out his plan.

Chapter 10

Many weeks later, when everyone was in their deep sleep and Burke was sure he would have no disruptions, he slipped out of bed and grabbed a flashlight. He made his way to the control center, finally, he had a chance of escape. Burke sat in the leather chair and switched on the first monitor. It beamed with light and he smiled to himself. *Finally! A computer!* He thought. He was tempted to ditch his plan and just play video games at the sight of this beloved object. Burke shook his head and got right to coding. If he wanted to be a gamer he would have to at least make it past fifteen.

I can't believe they didn't even put a password on these things. Burke shrugged and typed in more long strings of numbers and letters, looking for a hole in the system. He was trying to get the heavy metal doors unlocked. Burke zoned out from his surroundings as he coded, he even thought he could hear the sounds of street noise and screeching tires just like he was back home. He heard yelling and car doors slamming. His imagination was bringing him back to the city, and to his old life. Burke pressed enter and he heard a deadbolt slide out and click. "Yes!" He said aloud to himself. Another loud yell interrupted his celebration.

"Can those people just shut up!?"

Burke swiveled around and saw Sally standing in the doorway.

"What are you doing?" Burke hissed.

"Those people yelling woke me up." She replied with a shrug.

"Wait, you hear that too?"

"Isn't that what I just said?" Sally replied sassily.

"But I thought that was just my imagination." Burkes mind was racing. *Why are there people outside? Are they gonna raid us?*

"What are you doing anyway?" Sally walked over to the computer.

"I just unlocked the doors, we can get outta here now!" Burke replied excitedly.

"But I thought you liked Mom and Dad." Sally furrowed her brow in confusion.

"No! I was lying. They are seriously crazy and they should be arrested." Burke took Sally by the hand. "Let's go."

Sally clutched Burke's hand, running her other one along the wall. Burke had left his flashlight in the control room in his haste but didn't dare go back for it. They tried navigating their way through the dark halls, often running into walls and skirting around sharp corners.

When they finally reached the main shed door to the outside, Burke hesitated. "You ready?" He looked down at Sally. She gave a slight nod, he unlocked the door and slowly pushed it open. Bright sunlight filled the hall, momentarily blinding Burke. He stepped out into the cold morning air and looked around. His jaw dropped, dozens of men surrounded him, weapons raised. One stepped forward and squinted at Burke.

"What's your name?" The man shouted at him, his weapon aimed.

"Burke Rogers." Burke's voice cracked in fear, why were there so many people here? Were they here for him because he had hacked the computer?

"Where are your parents?" the man interrupted his thoughts.

Burke just stared blankly at him, frozen with fear. Burke read the small embroidered print on the man's uniform. *Lieutenant Phillips*, it said.

"Speak!" He commanded

C'mon Burke! His mind was telling him. "Why do you wanna know?" Burke finally said. "Are you gonna arrest them?" He asked.

Lieutenant Phillips chuckled. "Do you realize what they have done is highly illegal and is being considered as an attack against the United States? They have caused havoc to the entire continent, illegally messed with government owned property, and caused harm to our citizens of America? Arresting them would only be step one." Phillips finally lowered his gun.

"And how many steps are there?" Burke asked.

"Two." He replied, "Just two."

"What's the second?" Burke eyed Phillips' gun. "I think you can figure that out. I'm sure you know the penalty for treason." He finally said.

Burke gulped. *They're really crazy*, he thought to himself. *But they are my parents. They deserve to be arrested and incarcerated, but they can't be killed.* Burke looked around at all the men again, they had all lowered their weapons.

"Where are your parents?" The lieutenant asked again.

Burke said nothing.

"Fine. If you don't tell us we're going to find them anyway. Just don't get in our way or you could have the same fate as them." Lieutenant Phillips took another step forward and motioned to the others.

"No!" Burke ran to the door and blocked it with his body. "You can't kill them, they're my family!" Burke looked directly at lieutenant Phillips.

"Move it, kid." He snarled.

Burke shook his head. The lieutenant turned to his men and whispered something to them. Two stepped forward and grabbed Burke by his arms lifting him out of the way. Another took Sally by the hand and led her away. Burke kicked his legs and flailed his arms as he watched all the armed men duck into the first room. "You sure are a determined one." Lieutenant Phillips said to Burke as he slipped into the room.

Moments later Burke was pushed aside by the same men, this time coming out of the shed. Burke stood to the side of the door with Sally, watching the men drag his parents behind them. His parents tried to put up a fight but were soon tackled down by the large men.

The agent, Lieutenant Phillips, emerged from the shed, holding a key in his hand. Burke watched as he slowly turned the key in the door knob, he heard a soft click and the lieutenant pulled the key out of the door.

He turned and slipped the key into a plastic evidence bag. Burke was in a trance, watching a small ant on the ground race through the group of people.

Burke snapped back to attention as he heard the sputtering of a vehicle. He turned to watch the black government SUV pull out of the driveway. It skirted a sharp corner down the long road and Burke caught a glance of his parents in the back. He almost felt a sense of relief as he saw his parents go, but he was also angry at them. They were supposed to be loving and supportive parents, not crazy, evil criminals. Burke saw the faces of his parents again. They didn't have the sullen faces of newly captured prisoners, but instead, they wore identical broad smiles of triumph. Burke shivered. Maybe it was for the best that they were gone.

"I'm so sorry for your loss." A voice said as it came up behind Burke. He turned and saw the lieutenant approaching him.

"It wasn't really a loss," Burke said under his breath.

"Well, whatever you want to call it, kid." The lieutenant stood by Burke's side, his arms on his hips. Burke heard another set of footsteps, Sally came up on Burke's other side. She looked up at Burke and grinned, "Gotta go!" She said as she dashed off down the road at a surprising speed. Burke watched Sally run off, "Get back here!" He yelled after her. When she didn't even look back, Burke took off too, he couldn't just let his little sister run into the road like that.

"Hey! Where you going–" The lieutenant started to say but was cut off by a deafening explosion. Burke jumped, looked around but saw nothing. He jogged down the road and could make out the black SUV toppled over on its side. Smoke poured from the engine and the tires were deflated into piles of molten rubber. Burke stared at the scene, eyes wide, jaw agape. "Sally!" He cried. *Where did she go?*

"Burke!" He heard his name being called in a fierce whisper. He looked around for the source.

"Burke!" He heard again. Finally, he caught sight of a figure peeking out from behind the car. It was his mom. Burke shook his head and backed away.

"Let's go!" She beckoned for him. Burke looked around again. What other choice did he have? He leapt around the smoldering SUV and joined his parents.

"Wait!" He grabbed his dad's arm. "Where's Sally?"

Burke's dad smiled and gestured to the SUV.

"Hi!" Said another voice. It was Sally, emerging from the belly of the car, covered in soot and motor oil. She had a pair of wire cutters and a remote control in hand. "Dynamite." She said, holding up the remote.

"Now we can get outta here." She added with a triumphant grin.

THE END

CPSIA information can be obtained
at www.ICGtesting.com
Printed in the USA
BVHW032152210119
538337BV00001B/112/P